John

A Charge delivered in the Cathedral Fredericton

SALZWASSER
VERLAG

John

A Charge delivered in the Cathedral Fredericton

Reprint of the original, first published in 1859.

1st Edition 2022 | ISBN: 978-3-37512-162-4

Verlag (Publisher): Salzwasser Verlag GmbH, Zeilweg 44, 60439 Frankfurt, Deutschland
Vertretungsberechtigt (Authorized to represent): E. Roepke, Zeilweg 44, 60439 Frankfurt, Deutschland
Druck (Print): Books on Demand GmbH, In de Tarpen 42, 22848 Norderstedt, Deutschland

A CHARGE

DELIVERED IN THE CATHEDRAL,

FREDERICTON,

ON THURSDAY, SEPTEMBER 1, 1859,

TO THE

Clergy of the Diocese,

AND PUBLISHED AT THEIR REQUEST.

BY JOHN,
BISHOP OF FREDERICTON.

SAINT JOHN, N. B.
PRINTED BY BARNES AND COMPANY,
PRINCE WILLIAM STREET.
1859.

A CHARGE

DELIVERED IN THE CATHEDRAL,

FREDERICTON,

ON THURSDAY, SEPTEMBER 1, 1859,

TO THE

Clergy of the Diocese,

AND PUBLISHED AT THEIR REQUEST.

BY JOHN,

BISHOP OF FREDERICTON.

SAINT JOHN, N. B.
PRINTED BY BARNES AND COMPANY,
PRINCE WILLIAM STREET.
1859.

A CHARGE.

Reverend and Dear Brethren :

Though Triennial Visitations of the Clergy may be considered by careless and indifferent persons to be only a customary form, speedily discharged, and as speedily forgotten, no clergyman who knows his duty can so regard them ; least of all, I hope the person on whom the duty devolves of now addressing you. For I trust that none here present forget, that during the three years now past "the Lord of the vineyard" has looked for good fruit at our hands; that these years have taken away a part of the sum of life, of which, in many cases, but little remains ; and that we are all nearer to that dread account, which we must give of our ministry at the judgment seat of Christ. When we bear in mind St. Paul's description of what a Pastor should be ; when we read in Scripture the narrative of what the Apostle was; when our ordination vows meet us here, as it were, face to face, how can we think of our final account without fear and trembling? Nor do we meet to-day without other solemn recollections. The Venerable Archdeacon, whose kindly greeting, brotherly and valuable counsel were always extended to us on these occasions, is no more amongst us, and is himself gone to render that account which awaits all of us who remain. A promising and laborious young clergyman has found an early grave in a foreign land, and our little band has been still further reduced by other causes on which I need not dwell, but which may well make us "all tremble for the ark of God."

There are also grounds of peculiar anxiety, to which I must presently allude, which make me feel the burden of my cares especially heavy at this time. Our Church, and our people generally, may be said to be now on their trial; a trial which is likely to be prolonged for several years, and according to our behaviour under it, God will approve or condemn us, and posterity will either curse our apathy, or will "rise up, and call us blessed." We have a heritage to hand down unimpaired ; we have privileges of no ordinary kind to secure to others; we have a "sacred deposit" of truth to keep inviolate. We have to "take heed to this our ministry, that we fulfil it." Let us all, then, laying aside party spirit, party names, and party differences, betake ourselves with one mind and one voice to prayer, humbly beseeching our common Father in Christ, that He would bestow on us all "the spirit of counsel and might, the spirit of knowledge and of the fear of the Lord," that we may exhibit to the world that most edifying and convincing proof of the reality of our work, wise and godly counsel, and brotherly love. For however the gifts of one clergyman may be more attractive than those of another, however one may imagine that his views of the truth of the Gospel may be clearer than those of another, the common good of all can only be promoted by our unity in action, and those who do not belong to our communion, and many of those who are within it, will judge us, and will often judge the Church in which we are ministers, not by our party differences, but by our general conduct towards our flocks, and towards each other. And differences which seem important to us, are not held in much esteem by them. The more need then, that while we hold firmly what we have subscribed, and believe to be true, we should remember how many, on all sides, some of whom seem to have been holier Christians than ourselves, have held and taught differently.

Having made these general prefatory remarks, I now proceed to relate some of the facts, interesting to us and to our flocks, which have taken place during the last three years, and to suggest some reflections upon them, for our mutual benefit. And I shall also select a few other topics arising out of the difficulties of our position, or the peculiar circumstances of the times, on which I may venture some advice.

During the three years past, I have confirmed 1,333 persons, and have visited every Mission, and most of the Stations in the Diocese. I have also ordained twelve Priests and ten Deacons, have baptized many, both adults and infants, and have consecrated six Churches and four burial grounds. The number of persons confirmed is larger, the number of Churches consecrated smaller, than on former occasions. But the truth is, we have already more Churches than the clergy can properly supply, and we require a much more numerous body, to give to every station a full service once on the Lord's Day. Even this is less than is desirable. But how unsatisfactory is it to be obliged to give to any congregation no more than twelve services in the year, and of these often one-third, or more, on stormy days, when many are prevented from attendance? At present, however, we have no remedy but an occasional service during the week, and I think it is far better to take no more duty

on our hands than our strength will allow, and to perform that duty
regularly and efficiently, and not to multiply Churches beyond the
number which we can serve with regularity. I advise you, where
there are several Churches and Stations, to select one, the most
promising and important, to which your chief care should be given,
which may serve as a centre of operations, and may prevent your
work being frittered away by a number of services, which produce
no permanent effect. Where a clergyman has several services, I
strongly recommend a plan, which is found to answer well, and to
ensure a more punctual attendance. Let a list be printed, and
circulated among the parishioners at the beginning of the year,
containing every service, and the place and time of service. This
order should be, as far as possible, rigidly adhered to.

It seems not out of place here, to make a few remarks on the
important subject of Confirmation. I have before expressed my
views on the difficult question, the limit of requirement which we
should exact from the candidates for that holy rite. Two errors
are to be avoided. The one is, the discharging this duty hastily,
superficially, and with more regard to the numbers which can be
brought to be confirmed, than to an intelligent, serious, and holy
engagement on the part of the candidates themselves. It is no
time to seek out candidates for confirmation when the Bishop comes
into the parish, or into the neighbouring parish. The best way to
prepare the candidates is to make out a list of all the young people
of suitable age, at least a year beforehand. Time then will be
afforded for seeing them leisurely and privately, for ascertaining
their general habit of life, for suggesting to them their duty, for
pointing out to them Scriptures to be read, books of useful information, and for gradually removing from their minds needless scru-
ples or objections, which others are constantly setting before them.
It is distressing to witness, as I always do at times of Confirmation,
the exceeding pains which are taken to prevent young persons from
being confirmed. These attacks will be best met by anticipation,
which will prevent the young from being surprised by the mention
of objections. Another advantage which would arise from a longer
and more systematic preparation, is that the candidates would have
more time to consider their duty in regard to the Lord's Supper,
which many of them constantly neglect; and they would likewise
be more effectually taught that their engagement is of a binding
nature to the Church of England exclusively, and that they cannot
break this engagement, and fall away, as I fear too many do, into

the sin of schism.* They would also be led to take the step after earnest prayer to God for his help and guidance, with a thoughtful and humble desire to do right, as in the sight of God. And where we are satisfied that the spirit and intention are good, every allowance must be made for want of education, or defect of expression.

No doubt the kind of preparation, which I now recommend, will cost you a good deal of labour, but it is labour, not only well bestowed, but in the highest spiritual sense, remunerative. You will be more than repaid, if you can gather the younger members of the flock around you, and give them a permanent interest in the Church of England. One young man, well taught, and thoroughly grounded in his principles of duty, and prepared, by God's grace, to live as a consistent Churchman, will be worth more to you than a thousand hearers, who come to criticise and tolerate you, as long as you do not offend their prejudices, and who will desert you when offence is taken, and who never loved the Church, even when they professed to admire the pastor.

But whilst I urge upon you all the duty of assiduous preparation of the candidates for Confirmation, as well as of inculcating on them the duty of faithfulness to the Church, I also advise you not to exact from them too much. They are, for the most part, young and inexperienced, and cannot be expected to have attained that "ripeness and perfectness of age in Christ," which belongs to the advanced Christian. Professions of religious experience, and of the dealings of God with their own souls, are not to be trusted; and in most cases we cannot expect them to forego those recreations and amusements, in which their elders and betters have always (as they suppose) innocently joined. These are points on which good men will always differ. My own personal feeling has been rather unfavourable to such amusements, but experience has shown me that the rein cannot be drawn too tightly without danger of a reaction; and that if young people are not allowed to amuse themselves inno-

---

* Every thoughtful person must see, that, if it were generally understood that those who are confirmed, and who become Communicants in our Church, are at liberty to follow their own fancies in attending other places of worship, wheresoever and whensoever they please, there is an end to all steadfastness of principle—and if such a view be consistently followed, the pulpits of the Church of England ought everywhere to be open to divines of all persuasions, and on no account ought any of them to be re-ordained. In fact, Confirmation, under such circumstances, becomes an unmeaning form—a pretence of faithfulness never intended to be realized. Surely we can give others credit for sincerity and piety, without such vacillation. The clergy, by encouraging it, simply undo all their own work.

cently in the presence of their elders, they will amuse themselves by stealth, and with less restraint. And the great problem to be solved is, how to use all God's gifts without abusing them. Dancing, for example, is in itself no worse than running, playing at chess, or any other game of chance or skill, though, like all other recreations, it is easily capable of abuse. What is really objectionable is the unrestrained indulgence which sometimes accompanies it, as well as the lateness of the hour at which it is now fashionable to meet and separate. But my fear is, that if we exacted from every young person a pledge of abstinence from all such recreations, we should, if we could carry our point, only foster a morbid state of mind, or surround ourselves with persons who would deceive us, or themselves, or both. This question, no doubt, presents itself under a very different aspect to a young person in the town, and in the country. In the town, the pledge to abstain from such recreations is virtually an exclusion from ordinary society; in the country such an effect may not always follow. Whilst, therefore, a large margin may be allowed for discretion, my advice to you is, not to exact any pledges beyond what a fair and liberal construction of the promise made at the time of Confirmation seems to warrant, for the more pledges, the more snares to the conscience. At the same time, the small number of those who fulfil their vow, by partaking of the Lord's Supper, ought to be a very serious subject of reflection, and it is a matter of grave consideration, whether the custom of the Church in the United States, of admitting none to Confirmation who do not intend to communicate, be not better than our own. It has this obvious advantage, that the Pastor knows that those whom the Bishop confirms will strengthen his hands, when the Confirmation is over. On this point I feel that the counsel of my brethren will be of great advantage to me in forming a settled opinion, and in offering further advice.

This may be the proper place to add some remarks on the subject of Baptisms and Marriages. I hope you all discourage, as much as possible, the irregular practice of baptizing and marrying in private houses. I admit there are cases in which it is necessary. But the practice has extended itself to cases, in which it is not only unnecessary, but highly improper. No excuse can be alleged in towns for baptisms in houses, when the child is not really ill; and for marrying (in towns) in private houses at all. The Church is near at hand; the office requires that it should be performed in the Church; and you have all promised, before God, that you would minister the "discipline" of the Church (in which its rites must be included), "as this Church and realm hath received the same." *Necessity alone,* which cannot be pleaded when the Church is at hand, can exempt you from this duty. All that you require is, to let it be understood by Church-people generally, that such is your duty; that the Prayer Book, by which you are bound, and they ought to be guided, directs you how it is to be done, and that I, as required by the same Prayer Book, have called upon you so to do it. Obedience to our promises, when it is not done haughtily, pettishly, or capriciously, will command the respect of all reasonable people, and "obedience is better than sacrifice, and to hearken than the fat of rams." Every clergyman should also take care that a suitable book is provided for entering parochial baptisms, marriages and burials, and on no account should they be entered in a private memorandum book. Parochial registers are as much the property of the parish as parsonage-houses; and the certificate given to the civil Registrar of Marriages does not preclude the desirableness, on many accounts, of having our own registers. The accustomed form may be seen in the Cathedral library.

In performing the Marriage Service, it is not right, nor consistent with our duty, and our promise at ordination, that we should omit any part of it. We have as much right to leave out half the Litany, as to curtail the Marriage Service. And if there be any expressions in it which offend fastidious ears, or require explanation, the explanation can be given privately, or at a proper time, in public. But we are not responsible for these expressions; and we cannot expect others to follow our directions, if we ourselves set the example of disobedience to the Church. I also particularly recommend, that in every Church, in some convenient place, or in the vestry, a Table of Affinity, according to the Canons of the Church respecting Marriage, may be placed, that loose and irregular marriages may be prevented. It would also be very desirable, that in every Church where the seats are free, the fact should be recorded in some tablet kept in the vestry, or other convenient place, which will prevent disputes on the subject among the parishioners.

I may also observe, that it is not needful to bind yourselves to preach funeral sermons on every occasion of a burial. There are, no doubt, instances in which it may be very useful. But there are many, in which no notice could be taken of the departed, consistently with truth, without great pain to the surviving relatives, and in large parishes it becomes an unreasonable tax on your time and labour. At all funerals, every clergyman should appear in the dress of an officiating clergyman, that is, as the Church appoints, in a surplice.

It would be, I think, highly desirable that the meetings of Rural Deaneries should be held with more regularity. In some Deaneries much profitable intercourse, which might be had among the several members, has been suspended. An opportunity occurs at such times for Missionary Meetings, which might be most useful in promoting the objects of our Church Society, and in strengthening a spirit of godly zeal, and brotherly love, among all classes of your parishioners.

I am thankful to be able to report to you, that the Cathedral services have been kept up with unremitting attention, both during my residence and temporary absence in England, for the last three years. The attendance has been steady and good, and though since the death of the late venerable Archdeacon, I have been compelled to discontinue the afternoon service, I find no reason to be discouraged on the whole. The communicants, during the year now ending, have amounted to 2,231. Offertory collections are made at every Sunday service, and on all festivals, and though we have felt the pressure of the commercial crisis, they reached the sum of £331 19s. 9¼d., in the year 1858. More than £100 of this amount, however, was given to the Church Society, the Indian sufferers, the Clergy Mutual Insurance Society, the poor of the parish, and another special object. Of the remainder, the larger part was spent in providing light, fuel, attendance, repairs, sacramental wine, and other contingencies, leaving a small sum, £25, applied to the use of the officiating clergyman, and a small sum given to the Cathedral Endowment Fund. I am happy to add, that the largest collections made in any one Church in the Province for the Church Society, were made in the Cathedral. Thus far, then, God has helped us. And I may fairly ask the clergy to endeavour to urge their parishioners to increase their contributions in Church, at the half yearly collections throughout the Diocese. When I see, in the Annual Report, that our small population in Fredericton contributed upwards of £50, which is more than one-fourth of all the rest of the Diocese, you will agree with me, that there is reason for increase. In several Churches, no collection whatever is reported to have been made; in many, only one in the year. And out of fifty clergy, of whom only six or seven were curates, the names of only twenty-one appear in page 44 of the

B

Report, as having made collections in Churches for the Society. Making allowance for some possible error in the Report, I would earnestly press upon you, that this duty should be punctually discharged twice a year, either in June and October, as heretofore, or in any month which you deem more suitable than June, now that the time for the Annual Meetings has been altered to July; and that the collections, when made, should be transmitted, as soon as practicable, to the Treasurer. The steady advance of our annual subscriptions proves that the Society commends itself to the judgment and affections of all Churchmen; and to the unanimous support which it meets with from the clergy, much of its present prosperity is, no doubt, under God, to be ascribed. And it is peculiarly gratifying to find that, when so short a time has elapsed since our last Annual Meeting in January, no less than £1,000 should have been contributed in July; and the more so, as the change itself, the desirableness of which time only can show, was not likely at first to be productive of advantage to the interests of the Society.

Whilst, however, I call on you to thank God for his blessing thus vouchsafed, and congratulate you on the success of our joint exertions, it is only right that I should call your special attention, and the attention of the laity, to the position of our Church at this time, that we may see what our duty is, and may know how best to discharge it.

It has been very truly said, that our Church is a Missionary Church. No doubt it is exposed to many of the trials, and must encounter many of the roughnesses, inequalities, and hindrances of a missionary life. But this is not the whole aspect of it. Looking at the Statute-book, we see it called an Established Church. And while this expression has conferred on it very little, if any, advantage, it has exposed it to no small share of envy and obloquy. The Statutes of the time of king George the third, represent a state of government, and of general feeling in the community, which no longer exist. It is now no passport to office, no recommendation to politicians, that a man is a Churchman; no casual revenue is applied to the building of Churches. Yet the feeling, generated by the original system, that, somehow or other, Government takes care of the Church and the Clergy, still exists, and prevents many from seeing their duty to the Church, as it really is. This notion is also strengthened by our connection with our father-land, where an Established Church exists in reality; where tithes are paid for the support of the clergy, and rates levied for the repairs of the fabric, and where, in a large majority of parishes, the original or subsequent proprietors have given estates for the support of the Church. The parochial system there is a great blessing. Around the Church is a cluster of charities; alms left in perpetuity for poor and needy members; a school, it may be, wholly or partially, endowed, of which churchmen are trustees; a church population, more or less devoted to the ancient system, and blessed by traditionary recollections of their parents, grand-parents, perhaps their ancestors having been connected with the parish, and buried in the churchyard. Each successive parson, as the *persona ecclesiæ*, succeeds to this natural, orderly, and godly inheritance. The making or marring of the parish rests not with any single man. The poor look up to him as their guardian and protector, and with ordinary diligence and zeal, he is respected and beloved. The country clergy of this Diocese know how little there is, in this description, answering to their position. And yet emigrants, accustomed to these blessings from their infancy, find it hard to look their position steadily in the face, and act up to their duty. And as the natives of the Province have never seen the benefits of the old system, it is difficult to persuade them to provide what it is quite within their power to supply, so as to bring our parochial system somewhat nearer that of England. We have globes, which yield little; Churches without rates to maintain them; clergy without regular and systematic provision for their support; large territorial parishes more full of Dissenters than Churchmen; services required in more places than it is possible to visit; parishioners living at vast distances from each other, who ask for the same care, as if they were all gathered together comfortably and conveniently in one village; and by intermarriages, and want of instruction, the notions of a large number of our own people are altogether loose and indefinite. Hearing a good minister seems to be their sumnum bonum; "continuing in the Apostles' doctrine and fellowship, and in breaking of bread, and in prayers," is, I fear, made a secondary consideration. We have also a rigorous climate, and a long trying winter to contend with. The education, which we have hitherto been able to give to our children, has been, for the most part, of a most defective kind. The common schools, of necessity, furnish no guarantee for a religious education; and the clergy depend for the instruction they can give to the young on the Sunday School. Yet, too often, they have no time to attend to it themselves; and no Sunday School can flourish without their superintendance; for in every such institution there should be a thorough and systematic training, if possible, both of the teachers and the children. And the books used should be accommodated to the capacities of the scholars, and should be selected and approved by the clergyman. As, in short, this is, in many instances, your only opportunity of teaching them their religious duties and privileges, it behoves you to make the most of it, and if well done, it would lead to the practice, too fatally neglected, of public catechising.

Further: we are likewise surrounded by religious bodies, of whom I wish to speak with all possible respect, but of whom it cannot be said, with any show of justice, that they are friendly to our Prayer Book. "Master, so saying, thou reproachest us also," must apply to each one of them in turn, and we cannot avoid it. With all charity to them, we cannot make a new system, or unsay what we have all solemnly put our hands unto. Yet if the Reformation be a blessing, as we all believe it to be, some of our brethren must see themselves at fault; if our Prayer Book be one of the best fruits of that Reformation, those who have no Episcopacy must wish to vindicate their own position; and they whose founder with his dying breath, earnestly entreated them not to leave the Church of England, and threatened that " if they held meetings in Church hours, they should see his face no more;" must desire to show that they do not consider Church privileges worth the sacrifice. On the other hand, our solemn oath at ordination, our subscription before ordination, our constant preparation of candidates for confirmation, our refusal to open our Churches to ministers of other communions, and our re-ordination of those ministers when they conform ; customs which are no sign of particular parties in the Church of England, but are practised by all our Bishops, and by all our clergy in all parts of the world, show that we regard our position as not only tolerable, but as a *part of God's truth, founded on His holy word;* which it is our duty, however painful, steadfastly to maintain, until our protest is no longer required, and the breaches of the Church Catholic shall be (and God grant they may be) entirely healed.

Now, I say, that though our position may be a sound one, it is a position of no ordinary difficulty, and I am not surprised that we do not increase very largely : the wonder is, amidst so many discouraging and adverse circumstances, that we are able to hold our own, which unquestionably we do.

It ought to be remembered, also, that every expense connected with the fabric, or the services of the Church, falls upon the same persons, who are now called upon to support their own clergy, a fact which our brethren in England, who have so largely benefitted by the liberality of their ancestors, would do well to remember, more than some of them seem now disposed to do.

Hitherto, however, we have been assisted by a liberal pecuniary grant from the Society for Propagation of the Gospel. And though the largest sum allowed by that Society to its older Missionaries is far smaller than any layman, moving in a respectable sphere, would think sufficient to enable him to bring up a family upon, if he had no landed or other property to help him, yet, when counted as a whole, it undoubtedly amounts to a large sum of money. But, large or small, there is a general and, I believe, an increasing wish at home for its withdrawal. In the Diocese of Toronto no payments are any longer made. In Montreal they are in course of reduction. In Nova Scotia a fixed period is appointed for their withdrawal. And in Quebec and New Brunswick continual deductions are made from the sums formerly granted for the support of the clergy. From Trinity Church, and St. James, in St. John; from Fredericton, St. Andrews, Nelson, and Blackville, their assistance has been taken wholly; from Portland, Musquash, Prince William, Douglas, and Bathurst, a portion has been removed, and all other Missions, after any vacancy, by death or otherwise, must expect their turn of total loss or partial deprivation. A resolution of the Society, at one of its last public meetings, at which His Grace the Archbishop of Canterbury presided, re-affirms their determination, as regards the whole of British North America.*

Now, it would be madness not to see that such a determination on the part of those who have assisted us with great kindness for a long time, and who have a right to say how their money shall be employed, provided good faith be kept, involves us (as a Church) in very serious responsibility. Either we must provide for the support of our Churches, and of the ministers who serve them, and provide creditably and speedily, or our Missions must in many cases be abandoned. Let all Churchmen consider what must follow the abandonment of any Mission, if even a poor country Mission.

---

* I thought it right to protest, when in England last year, against the withdrawal or diminution of the grant made by the Society, in case of exchange of Missions by two clergymen, which act only subjects them and ourselves to serious inconvenience, but seems to me wholly uncalled for. We all understand, that after death, a reduction is to be made.

The Church is closed. The parsonage is shut up. The usual regular round of services and sacraments is discontinued. The Sunday School no longer assembles under the approving eye, and cheerful superintendance of its proper guide. The inspired word is no longer publicly read. Irregular habits are formed. Prayer is neglected, and the young begin to pass the Lord's Day in listless idleness or dissipation ; or if more serious, they often join another Communion. Children die without baptism. Sufferers linger on in pining sickness, longing for the well-known footstep and familiar voice of their pastor, but no one comes to read and pray, and console them. Or if a visit be paid, a new system is to be learned, the Prayer Book is laid aside as useless, their baptism is disallowed, their whole mind is disquieted, and being assured that their life has been all wrong, and their convictions of truth an entire delusion, trembling on the verge of eternity, they renounce their baptism, swallow with credulity a new faith, wild with fear and excitement, and turn their backs on all that they have held dear in religion. Meanwhile, the Church or Churches, to which we have all contributed, which the Societies at home have liberally aided, to which the parishioners have pointed with pleasure and with pride, as the fruit of their labours, fall into decay; the parsonage is occupied by others, the whole parish is a moral ruin. And who can think without horror of the multiplication of this evil, and of the desolation and waste of God's heritage, which it is given us to preserve, to build up, to enlarge and beautify, not to destroy ? These souls are, it is true, at present under the charge of one appointed pastor, but they are all our joint care, and no single member of the Church of England in this Province has a right to say that he does not care for them. Nor is this the only evil connected with the abandonment of Missions. The social loss may, perhaps, come home to some minds, which would not be suitably affected by the spiritual evil. In our remote country Missions, the pastor is sometimes the best educated man in a considerable district; he has sympathies and feelings not wholly confined to the narrow spot of ground on which he moves; he is desirous, as far as he is able, to refine the taste, and soften the asperities of his neighbours, and diffuse a larger measure of intelligence amongst them, by means of religious and useful publications. He lends his aid and countenance to all useful and industrial undertakings, and is a foremost man in the work of general education. If he be a married man, (and St. Peter, whom our Roman Catholic brethren hold up to us as their head and pattern, was "himself a married man,") the domestic influences of a married priest are of no small use in softening the difficulties of a parish. His wife is, or ought to be, foremost in assisting her husband in ministering to the sick and the poor, and many acts of sympathy may be performed by her which money cannot purchase, and which bind the hearts of the parishioners to herself and her husband. All these influences for good—socially, morally, spiritually—are withdrawn, and every one is left to take care of himself.

But it may be said, what is the remedy? Can it be expected that a poor country should supply incomes for fifty clergy, and should make up a deficiency, which must amount to many thousand pounds? It cannot be expected, certainly, that poor men should do this. But it is expected, nay, it is the positive duty of the wealthy Churchmen in New Brunswick, whether their money have descended to them by grants of land from the Crown, or has been made by God's blessing on their abilities and industry in the legal profession, in mercantile pursuits, in agriculture, or in any other honourable way of life, to provide liberally for the spiritual wants of their less wealthy brethren in this Province. This is a duty which all ages have acknowledged, which the founders of our common Christianity recommended; which cannot be neglected without subverting the foundation of religion itself. One noble example of such liberality, arising, I firmly believe, from a profound conviction of duty, and from no meaner motive whatever, was set by the late Chief Justice, but has been followed only in three or four instances, as far as my knowledge extends. But what we now require is not a few isolated instances of generosity, but a general contribution, arising from a general sense of duty. We do not appeal merely to wealthy merchants and landowners in St. John, but to every Churchman who has a stake in the country, to all who sincerely love their Church and their religion, and fear their God, and we say, on you rests the fearful responsibility of continuing or of destroying the services of the Church of England in this Province. The crisis, long expected, is now come. The funds raised by the Church Society, though large and increasing, are not capable of bearing this great burden. You must now do as your ancestors in England did, endow the Church in perpetuity for the public good, nay for your own good, and the good of your children after you. We do not dictate to you the amount which you should give, nor the manner in which your offering should be applied. But it will be a disgrace to the Church of which you are members, to the country which sustains you, it will be unfortunate for your reputation, if you allow the Church to perish, or to be materially weakened, by refusing to extend a liberal hand in this emergency. And we call on you, on strictly Scriptural principles, to do this. The clergy of this Province do not ask for large incomes, and luxurious fare. They ask only for necessaries. They require that they should have an income which, with prudence and strict economy, will keep them free from debt. And they require assistance in the education of their children, where they are married and have offspring. And unless some plan be adopted, which will either raise the income of the Church Society to the amount necessary to meet these claims, or an Endowment Fund be raised, the Missions in poor districts must, in a very few years, be abandoned altogether.

Already, the scantiness of the incomes of the clergy has begun to react on the ministry, and for the first time in my Episcopate I am unable at present to fill the vacant Missions for want of men.

In Nova Scotia, they have already begun to act on these convictions. Not only has the sum of £10,000 been raised by Churchmen in that colony for the Collegiate Institution at Windsor, but a large sum has been already subscribed for an Endowment Fund, and collections are being made in various parts of the country for this object, and the amounts are very considerable. I do not believe that, in our case, the means are deficient, and I hope the will to perform will not be wanting. Only let the magnitude of the object be duly felt, and we shall find means to compass it. It is not necessary that we should adopt every rule laid down by our brethren in Nova Scotia, but that we should act, and act promptly, is not only desirable, but necessary, I may say, to our existence as a spiritual society. In any plan of operations, I should be desirous of being assisted by your advice, and by that of laymen of judgment and experience; and it might be deemed proper that a committee should be named to advise with me on this important subject, and that measures should be taken to bring this matter distinctly before the minds of the members of our communion.* But let this be remembered by all concerned, that we require nothing which Holy Scripture does not recommend, and which St. Paul does not enjoin upon all his flocks.

---

* If any question should be raised respecting the patronage of benefices endowed by the laity, I should be perfectly willing that such benefices should be placed in the presentation, or alternate presentation, of the families who endow. But the laity must remember, that the difficulty in these cases, would not lie with me, but with the Crown.

If the Apostle for a season abstained from taking contributions from the Corinthians, and wrought with his own hands to support himself, it was to deprive a wealthy and luxurious people of matter of accusation against him, rather than his customary practice, or that of his fellow Apostles; and in these days working with our hands for our support, would be simply so much time and thought taken from the people who require our care.

I also hope that, in all our works of charity we shall bear in mind that whatsoever is given, in order to its acceptance, must be given as an offering of love to God. It is on this ground that the Church of England rests the offertory. Our alms are collected in time of public worship, when we meet together to confess our sins before God, obtain his pardon, strengthen our faith, and show forth its fruits. Having been collected by "deacons, or other fit persons," they are brought to the priest, who offers them to God as the fruit of our faith and love at his table, beseeching him to accept, for Christ's sake, both them, and our souls and bodies, as "a willing sacrifice." And the sentences appointed to be read are of such a kind as absolutely forbid the supposition, that the Church ever intended that the money so collected should be applied exclusively to the poor. For several of the sentences relate wholly to the support of the ministry; as for example, the following: "If we have sown unto you spiritual things, is it a great matter if we shall reap your carnal things?" "Who feedeth a flock, and eateth not of the milk of the flock?" "Even so hath the Lord ordained, that they who preach the Gospel should live of the Gospel." This offering is called by St. Paul "the sacrifice and service of our faith." And though this does not prevent our giving at other times and in other ways, yet it shows us in what manner of spirit we should be when we give to God. My reverend brethren will, I trust, pardon me, if I respectfully, but decidedly, express my hope, that they will re-consider the subject of offerings made for Churches, and other charitable objects, and remembering that the word of God is our only rule of faith, will examine for themselves how far bazaars, and other such modes of collecting money, can be considered scriptural methods of gathering the alms of the faithful. Can it be pretended that anything at all resembling such a procedure is recommended or permitted in Holy Scripture? St. Paul's directions for charitable objects are brief, but emphatic and comprehensive; that "on the first day of the week each one should lay by in store as God hath prospered him," and he adds, that this godly custom of sepa-

c

rating a part of our incomings for religious uses, should be observed both in the Churches of Galatia and Corinth. The Apostle, in short, speaking by the Spirit of God, "*ordains*" it.* Have we any right to alter or abolish it, or substitute another method for it? Bazaars are, doubtless, a most convenient mode of raising a large sum of money, easily, and at once. But how much more acceptable in God's sight may we suppose that such an offering would be, if the work were begun, continued, and ended in Him, and humbly presented as the fruit of our deep conviction of his immeasurable love, and of our deep unworthiness? The trade carried on at a bazaar, the amusement, the refreshments for the body, the mirth and raillery, are perfectly innocent in ordinary life, but they are not part of our charity, nor of our worship. Nor are they meet to take the place of charity in any place which is to be immediately dedicated to God's honour and worship. And as they take their standard from the world, they partake of the lowness of the associations of the world. The objects to which all eyes are directed are money and amusement. How perfectly out of place, at such a time, would it appear, if the assembled crowd were summoned to partake of the Lord's Supper, or to listen to the seventeenth chapter of St. John's Gospel! Yet if we meet to offer ourselves and our substance to the Lord, these sweet memorials of his dying love, would be entirely in season, and like Manoah's sacrifice, our alms would ascend in the flame of the altar. Imagine, in such a promiscuous crowd, bartering their wares, the venerable Apostles coming in, to receive and present to their Divine Master, the holy and united offering of these Christians' love. The men and the words seem misplaced. And when we see, instead of these high and heavenly motives, the lowest animal instincts of our nature occasionally appealed to, I wonder how people can imagine that

---

* "*As to season*—'upon the first day of the week.' The Christian Sabbath Day, the day of the Lord's resurrection, and of spiritual invigoration and progress. *As to persons*—'Let every one of you,' old and young, rich and poor, all possessing any personal means. *As to method*—'Lay by him in store.' Place it in a sacred treasury, ready for occasons of use. *As to measure*—'As God hath prospered him,' according to the gains and mercies of the week. *As to the principle of this method*—'That there be no gatherings when I come.' No need for appeal to inferior motives; but that all may be provided beforehand, as of conscientious purpose and bountiful devotion; and may, consequently, exceed in measure and moral worth the combined results of all other methods, being the result of the loftiest principle, and the full aggregate of all that ought in justice to be so employed." Essay, by the Rev. J. Ross, a Nonconformist Minister, in "Gold and the Gospel," p. 275.

they can preserve in their minds a sense of what is due to God, when they make an offering to him. To a Christian every act of his life ought to be an act of worship. His rising from rest, his private prayers, his daily meals, his family devotions, his attention to business, his very recreations, his alms, and all the actions of his life, are consecrated by prayer and thanksgiving; and no part of his duty is more solemn than his rendering back to God a portion of these gifts, which Christ purchased with his precious blood, and of which, "when the Son of Man shall come in his glory, and all the holy angels with him," he will say, if offered in faith and love and holiness, "Inasmuch as ye have done it unto the least of these my brethren, ye have done it unto me." I beg you to understand, that these words are not meant as censure of what any of you may have been led to do in your extremity, by the advice and offers of others. I take it for granted, that no clergyman would prefer to collect his money by a bazaar in preference to a more Scriptural method. It is resorted to when charity languishes, and other methods fail. I am fully aware of the difficulties under which you labour, the low tone of society in general, the tempting offers made to you by the laity, the certainty of finishing great and good works, in which you are deeply interested. But pardon me if I observe, that building of Churches is only one of the means to a great end; and the end is the building up of living temples of the Holy Ghost. The end is the inculcation of the highest motives by the means which the Word of God proposes, and by no others; lower motives may build Churches, but will not save souls.*
And if you encourage men to give on the lower principle, it will be much more difficult to raise them to the higher. For the world is an apt scholar in lowering of motives. There are people enough already who come to Church for amusement, and regard us, and all our proceedings, as little better than the acts and actors in a play. What I have now said, however, I have said only from the desire of conforming strictly to the Scripture, and of recommending to you what I shall have no need to blush for when I hear it again as part of my own work, at the great day of account.† I pass to other topics, which I cannot leave untouched.

---

* It was by the sale of indulgences for the purpose of building St. Peter's Church in Rome, that so much evil was done before the Reformation.

† After having written my Charge, I lighted upon some remarks in a small work by Mr. H. Taylor, a very elegant and philosophical writer, which are so apposite, that I make no apology for extracting them. "There are some

If I do not say much now on the subject of the manner of performing the rites of the Church, reading Holy Scripture publicly, and preaching, it is not that I am less sensible of their great importance (I hope I am far more sensible of it), but that having dwelt so often on these subjects, I am unwilling to repeat myself. Yet I would particularly beseech the younger clergy to remember how much just cause of complaint they give to others, if they perform any part of the service in an irreverent manner, and that inattention to small things, as well as to great, mutilation of the services, hurrying the prayers and lessons, carelessness in regard to the Lord's Supper, slovenliness in any holy actions, must convey to others the idea, that we are not thoroughly in earnest. Can any one of us conceive the injury which an inattentive, irreverent, apathetic, negligent clergyman does to mankind?

In this view, how really fearful are the words of the ordination service! "If it shall happen that the same Church, or any member thereof, shall take any hurt or hindrance by reason of your negligence, ye know the greatness of the fault, and also the horrible punishment that will ensue." These are words which may make the holiest tremble, and should wring with anguish the heart of a careless or negligent clergyman. For if he do not tremble and "repent, and do the first works"—then God help him, he is wholly lost.

---

other ways of the world, in this matter of charity, which proceed, I think, upon false principles and feelings,—charity dinners, charity balls, charity bazaars, and so forth; devices (not even *once* blessed) for getting rid of distress without calling out any compassionate feeling in those who give, or any grateful feeling in those who receive. God sends misery and misfortune into the world for a purpose; they are to be a discipline for His creatures who endure, and also for His creatures who behold them. In *those* they are to give occasion for patience, resignation, the spiritual hopes and aspirations which spring from pain when there comes no earthly relief, or the love and gratitude which earthly ministrations of relief are powerful to promote. In *these* they are to give occasion for pity, self-sacrifice, and devout and dutiful thought, subduing, for the moment at least, the light, vain, and pleasure-loving motions of our nature. If distress be sent into the world for these ends, it is not well that it should be shuffled out of the world without any of these ends being accomplished; and still less that it should be made the occasion of furthering ends in some measure opposite to these; that it should be danced away at a ball, or feasted away at a dinner, or dissipated at a bazaar. Better were it, in my mind, that misery should run its course with nothing but the mercy of God to stay it, than we should thus corrupt our charities. Let me not be misunderstood. Feasting and dancing, in themselves and by themselves, I by no means disparage; there is a time and a place for them; but things which are excellent at one time and occasion, are a mere desecration at another. It is much more easy to desecrate our duties than to consecrate our amusements; and better, therefore, not to mix them up with each other."—Taylor's "Notes from Life," p. 15. Murray, 1854.

With regard to sermons, I have in former addresses offered advice on the best mode of composition, on their length, on the variety of topics which they should embrace. On such matters I hope to be always learning something useful to the end of my life. And the subject is so important, that I may be excused for adding some brief remarks on the present occasion.

1. We must recollect, that a higher standard of preaching is required of us than of our predecessors, in consequence of a more generally diffused education. Our hearers are always more disposed, and are in some cases more competent to criticise, than they were in former days. And many of them have volumes of good, original sermons in their possession, by which our efforts in the same direction may be tested. Sermons on mere general subjects—such as the happiness of the righteous, and the misery of the impenitent—will not now be interesting or useful. There must be a fulness in the treatment of doctrine, an aptness at explanation of places of Holy Scripture, an unction in speaking of holy things, and an earnestness and reality of speech, or our efforts will be little valued.

2. The time given by our hearers to serious thought is after all very short. If you consider the necessary business of your people, their temptations, and their hindrances to devotion, the many Sundays when they stay at home, or are sick, and that one half hour is all they allow us to give to an earnest address on the subject of religion, how unspeakably important it is that we should make the best of that short time, and send them away with something to reflect upon! some warning driven home, some "nail fixed in a sure place," some promise cheeringly made clear, some doctrine powerfully and practically enforced on their attention. In every sermon the preacher should aim at a definite object. The whole Gospel is so vast and complicated a scheme, that the attempt to bring in every part of it at once must be a failure, and must end in meaningless phrases, which are not practically useful. And whatever be our subject, if it be Scriptural, and the foundation on which we build be sound, the Gospel is preached, as indeed it was preached by our Lord in the sermon on the Mount, though neither the atonement, nor justification by faith were directly named therein. Yet it would be impossible to mention a grace there recommended, in which both these doctrines are not implied.

3. In the preparation of your sermons, as well as in reading the second lessons, I particularly advise you always to make use of the

original Greek. However faithful be our translation, (and of its general accuracy there can be no reasonable doubt,) a sound exposition of Scripture is impossible without reference to the original, for without it we often misunderstand the translation, and we constantly misread it. And in the Gospels and Epistles (especially in the Epistles of St. Paul,) there are niceties of expression, and shades of meaning, which no foreign tongue can express, and which, therefore, no translation can convey to the mind of the reader. What translation can reach the force of the words in the 12th chapter of the Epistle to the Romans, rendered "kindly affectioned one to another with brotherly love," or "not slothful in business," lazy in your speed; or of the testamentary covenant in the 9th chapter of the Hebrews, or of the being "offered on the sacrifice and service of your faith," in the Epistle to the Philippians, his pouring out his life's blood as a drink offering upon the sacrifice and liturgical prayers of his faithful converts, his martyrdom being well rewarded by their conversion ?* And what but the Greek can be our guide in the double emphasis of "Lord dost *thou* wash *my* feet" —the word "my" being transposed from its usual place in the sentence for the purpose of emphasis ? It is true that salvation may be had without the understanding of these, and similar forms of speech, but in us, as teachers of the word, a far more accurate knowledge is required than in laymen. And unless we possess that knowledge, how can we meet and answer with solidity and force the heresies which prevail, the ever-varying forms of error on all sides, the wrestings of Holy Scripture, the building piecemeal upon single texts, men "worshipping their own imaginations," and neglecting the great body of revealed truth ? The popular taste is satisfied with a very shallow theology. The repetition of a few leading doctrines, the announcement of a few stereotyped phrases, a pleasing utterance, friendly manner, earnest way of preaching, and diligent visiting, are in its judgment, sufficient to make the divine. But far more than this is required of those who would bring forth out of their "treasures things new and old." I strongly recommend to you to secure, as a help to your studies, Dr. Wordsworth's Commentary on the New Testament. It possesses qualifications not found in equal fulness in any Commentary with which I am acquainted. You will find in it:—1. The deepest reverence for the inspiration of Scripture, of which many have lax and defective

---

* The Greek words are necessarily omitted for want of type.

views. 2. A great insight into the spiritual meaning of Scripture, with a careful adherence to its literal facts. 3. An ample store of patristic learning, and of the admirable comments of our Reformers and other chief Anglican Divines, as well as copious references to larger works. 4. A full discussion on critical points, especially on questions of chronology, and the authorship and object of the several portions of the inspired writings. 5. A fuller illustration of the meaning of many difficult texts than is to be found in most other commentators, as far as my knowledge extends; and 6, which I deem especially desirable, the reader is not perplexed often (as is the case in other Commentaries) with a vast multitude of interpretations. 7. The whole is conceived in a charitable, moderate spirit, with a decided loyalty towards the Church of England. The addition of maps would make this invaluable to every clergyman, and it is greatly to be desired that it may be found practicable to reduce its price.

4. One word more, and I detain you no longer on this subject. It is of the highest importance to the whole community, that you should keep watch over the style in which your sentences are composed. Living as we do so near the border land, where corruptions of every kind are found, and are imported among us, we must beware lest we fall unawares into common place vulgarity. Already, the occasional language even of public speakers defies all grammar, and belongs to no known tongue; and it will require all our care and diligence to preserve that wholesome Saxon, of which our Bible translation supplies so rare and noble an example. For this purpose, I recommend to you all the philological works of the Dean of Westminster, most of which are published in a cheap form in the United States, such as Trench on the "Study of Words," "English past and present," "the Synonymes of the New Testament," his work on "Proverbs," and his "Glossary of English Words." The study of these little works will give you information which cannot readily be obtained from any other source, and will help to purify and invigorate your style, and make it intelligible, manly, and chaste.

I come now to a far less pleasing topic, which I would gladly have passed by, had I deemed it consistent with my duty so to do. Since we last met, several cases have occurred among the clergy, which have given me unusual anxiety and pain. But I must do the great body of those whom I address the justice to say of them, that not only in their own lives are they exempt from reproach, but that they earnestly desire that the discipline of the Church should be firmly and temperately maintained. My own course in reference to such matters has been founded on the following principles, which I submit to you are reasonable and sound, though I will not undertake to say that I have been faultless in the application.

1. It is clearly not my duty to seek for matter of accusation against any of the clergy, nor to procure evidence against them. Complaints, if made, should proceed from one of their own body, or of the laity of their parishes, as are officially charged with the duty of watching over the interests of the Church.

2. I am bound not to receive any accusation except in writing, signed by responsible parties, and capable of being supported by sufficient evidence, of which the accused should have full notice.

3. If no charge be brought before me officially, but the facts are admitted by the offender, I must be allowed to deal with the matter as I deem best for the interests of the Church, after taking the best advice I can obtain.

4. I hold that no clergyman should be deprived of his office for any single offence, which does not amount to a high degree of criminality. Every one is entitled to the benefit of repentance and amendment of life, and I differ wholly from such as have censured me for not proceeding at once to harsh and rigorous measures against some who have offended. And I am prepared, privately or publicly, before God and man, to justify my own course of proceeding herein. But one thing is undeniable, that no offence or scandal has ever remained long unredressed by me since I came to the Diocese, and that in almost every instance in which I have been charged by some with negligence or too great indulgence, in the selfsame cases others have considered my conduct harsh and hasty. Both charges cannot at the same time be true : and my conscience bears me witness, that I have endeavored to avoid both errors ; but I dare not affirm that I have done so with uniform success. But let my accusers remember that they themselves are men ; and above all, let them not visit my supposed offence on the Church to which we all belong, and by these means, even if I be wrong, publicly condemn themselves. For how can it be the duty of any to mark their sense of a Bishop's error, by committing another fault in their own persons ? Two faults surely do not make one virtue.

The faults of others ought to be regarded by us all as so far our own, as we are members of one body ; and " if one member suffer all the members must suffer with it." Let us all learn from such misfortunes humility, watchfulness, and tenderness of soul; let our prayers be daily offered up, not only for ourselves, but for each other, that we may all walk worthy of our high vocation, serving the Lord " with all humility and singleness of heart," that we " may stand perfect and complete in all the work of God."

In common with yourselves, I lament that two clergymen, lately beneficed in this Diocese, have been so ill advised, as, after leaving it, openly to connect themselves with the Irvingite sect. Neither of them had publicly avowed his opinions before he left us, and though I was aware of the tendency in one of the cases alluded to, I hoped that my leniency and forbearance would have led to a different result. Nothing however occurred before their departure which would have warranted me in proceeding publicly against either of them. Their position is now totally altered. Residing in the Diocese of Toronto, they have no license from the Bishop, and are both schismatically ministering to certain followers of their party, in direct violation of their ordination vows. Having lately paid a visit to this Province, they proceeded to circulate a pamphlet among the clergy, the statements of which are quite sufficient to condemn them; and they endeavoured to unsettle the minds of some of the laity by introducing the subject of their peculiar doctrines. I was compelled therefore to refuse to admit them to the Holy Communion, and I now enjoin the same course upon yourselves; and I trust that after this public declaration, no laymen will allow them to make use of their hospitality as a means of disseminating their dangerous errors. The sect to which they belong was first formed under the ministry of the Rev. Edward Irving, a Presbyterian, who imagined that it had pleased God to revive the miracle of Pentecost, by inspiring some of his followers to speak with new tongues. On examination by the learned, it was discovered that the new language resembled no other in existence, and consequently could be of no possible use in the conversion of the heathen; and that, on this account, instead of being " a sign to unbelievers," which was the object of the Pentecostal gift, it was a sign, if real, only to those who possessed it. It was at length confessed by a convert* to be nothing more than a putting together of a jumble of English letters, so as to wear the appearance of an unknown tongue; a most certain indication of delusion, either purely mental, or Satanic, and it seems now to have worn itself out, as we

---

* Mr. Baxter.

hear little said about it. These enthusiasts were not however satisfied with a claim so easily detected by the learned. They further gave out, that they were called by God to revive the Apostolate. Such of them as pretended to be prophets, called on others to take on themselves the office of Apostles, and at length twelve men were set apart for this office, who reside, I believe, most of them in England, and are some of them, undoubtedly, engaged in secular callings.

No one can fail to see how entirely opposed this is to the calling of the Apostles in the New Testament. All the first twelve were called immediately by our Lord, when he was on earth. After the death of Judas, St. Matthias was chosen by Divine interposition, ("show whether of these two THOU hast chosen,") and St. Paul was called by a Divine manifestation from heaven. No other persons pretended to the same peculiar call. The Apostles confined themselves strictly to the work of the ministry and appointed deacons, that they might not "serve tables." But in what passage of the New Testament is there any indication that another body of twelve would again be Divinely chosen? The Apostles were called by Christ. These persons were nominated by their friends, and ascribed it to the Holy Ghost. The Apostles all spake with tongues, foreign, indeed, to the Jews of Jerusalem, but perfectly intelligible to those whom they addressed. These pretenders to the Apostolate do not all speak even in the one unintelligible tongue, which proves to be a jumble of broken English. The Apostles went everywhere, "the Lord working with them, and confirming the word by signs following," in presence of multitudes of the heathen. One of the leading pretended Apostles, confines his labors chiefly to the British Senate, where we hear of him filling men's mouths with laughter at his witty speeches. Such is their Apostolate; founded on a gross delusion in its origin, and tending to the subversion of all order and authority in the Church of God, under the guise of reverence for the Church.* Mixed with this, we find prophecies of the speedy coming of Christ at a definite time, contrary to the express declaration of our Saviour, that "of that day and hour knoweth no man, no, not the angels in heaven, but my Father only." I need say no more to induce you

---

* Though great respect is paid outwardly to the Episcopal office by such persons, yet it soon ceases, when any difference arises between us and themselves; and it is then manifest that the "Apostles" claim to inherit all the prerogatives of Vicars of Christ as truly as the Pope of Rome.

to beware of the attempts of such men. And I believe we are not passing the limits of charity if we say, that we fear they are like those whom St. Paul describes as "false Apostles, deceitful workers, transforming themselves into the Apostles of Christ." But I trust that "their folly shall be manifest unto all men," as that of other deceivers was. And it is remarkable, that this modern delusion, like all others, has its counterpart in ancient days. Tertullian's account of Priscilla and Montanus, and their followers, closely resembles the pretensions of the deluded followers of Edward Irving, who, indeed, died repenting of his illusions and mistakes.

I cannot wholly pass by another instance of error, which unhappily excites more attention. And though this Diocese is happily free, and I earnestly trust will continue to be free from similar instances of perversion, yet as our late friend and associate seems disposed to "busy himself in other men's matters," and intrude into places where he has no call, I may be excused from adding a few words on his case. To my mind, who have always been nursed in the bosom of our beloved and honored Church, and distinctly cherish the remembrance of an earnest wish, at the age of five years from my birth, never afterwards intermitted, to enter her holy ministry, his account of his ordination, life, and conversion to Rome, appears perfectly suicidal. I do not pretend to understand the feelings of any man, who could allow himself to be ordained, standing in doubt, where the Church required him to promise, and where he did promise, that he stood in no doubt whatever. I do not comprehend how any man, still doubting, could allow himself to be summoned by the laity of the Church in Halifax, to be their special champion against the Church of Rome, and also could deliberately print his convictions of the errors of that Church. Nor do I see how any man, sincerely attached to the Communion which he still professed to love, could resort for secret help to its professed enemies, and never to its many learned defenders, any of whom would have been ready to help him. But I still less understand how any man of judgment and sense, can expect men of sense to listen to him, when he informs us in his second pamphlet, p. 13, that his conversion was owing to his witnessing the funeral of the late Archbishop of Halifax, and describes the "slow and solemn procession, the long train of ecclesiastics, the chanting of the psalms, *the fragrance of the incense,* the lighted tapers, and elevated cross," as incidents tending to the sudden change in his mind. When a man is so weak as to allow *even his sense of perfumes* to be pressed into the service as a motive for his conversion, I really hope there is sufficient common sense left among us to reject his proposals.

His arguments in general must have something better in them than this, or no one would read them; but I observe of them all, that there is not one which has not been often urged, and as often refuted. In Bishop Gibson's most valuable work, "Preservative against Popery,"—being a collection of tracts written by the most learned of our Divines in the times of James the second—you will find every one of Mr. Maturin's arguments solidly and admirably answered by anticipation. And there is nothing in his pamphlet which is not set forth with all the elegance of graceful verse by Dryden, in his "Panther and Milk-white hind." Indeed, if the controversy have changed at all since 1688, it has changed, as I conceive, in our favour; partly because the Church of England has exhibited so many and striking evidences of internal life and holiness, of external development and progress, and of all the signs of the Divine blessing which accompany and follow such a manifestation;* and partly, because the Church of Rome has added another astounding proof, that she is not ashamed to require as an article of faith what the Scriptures no where teach, what the creeds of the Catholic Church no where contain, what the ancient doctors and martyrs expressly disavow, what the most eminent Romish writers of later date steadfastly deny, and therefore, to use Mr. Maturin's words, she is, out of her own mouth, convicted " of having contradicted herself in an article of the faith which she has now positively defined," and has placed herself in open opposition to Scripture, reason, and testimony.

---

* "It is only forty-five years since the first Missionary landed among the cannibals of New Zealand. It is only twenty years since the Colony was formed. Yet, on the 5th March, 1859, the first meeting of a General Synod of our Church was held, at which four Bishops, the representatives of sixty clergymen, and lay deputies representing several thousand laity, were present. During the Synod another Bishop was consecrated, making the fifth; and a sixth was shortly expected to be appointed to take charge of the work in the Melanesian Islands."—Church Journal.

"In the year 1818, only 41 years since, only three Colonial Bishops had been consecrated—one for Nova Scotia, one for Quebec, and one for Calcutta. Six were consecrated for the United States, and thirty-two for England and Scotland. In 1858 these numbers are swelled to 114 Bishops, presiding over the same territories, so that our numbers are (within nine) trebled; and in forty years more, if no check be experienced, they will, at the same rate of increase, amount to 342, a larger number than met in Synod at Nicæa." And the multiplication of the clergy and laity will, I doubt not, keep pace with their increase. —Christian Remembrancer, for January, 1859.

It is not my intention to enter fully into the controversy, for several reasons. 1. This offending clergyman was not in my jurisdiction, but in that of my revered brother, who has already dealt with the case as he saw fit: and 2. Mr. Maturin's first pamphlet has already met with a full and convincing answer, written by one of our own body, to whom I desire to return my own thanks, publicly, for his well-timed and very able defence of our Church against an ingenious, and in spite of all his apparent charity, a very unsparing adversary. Mr. Maturin's pamphlet will do good service in one respect, whatever evil it may do in others. It must be evident to all thinking men among us, that we can have no place with Rome, because her motto is "Delenda est Carthago." Her openly avowed policy is to rise on the ruins of us all. She allows neither the validity of our baptism, nor of our orders, nor even of our faith; we are treated simply as heathens. "There is no real alternative," says Mr. Maturin, p. 85, "between the principle of *infallibility*, and the principle of *infidelity*." Either then we must believe all that the Roman Church now teaches as matter of faith, (and we can prove by incontestible evidence, that our adversaries themselves did not believe it all six years ago, for the immaculate conception of the Virgin Mary was not then defined to be an article of faith,) or (as we are told) we believe nothing. Such is the frightful alternative afforded to our acceptance, by one who, for eighteen years, ministered at our altars, and repeated, in common with ourselves, that ancient creed to which an Œcumenical Council forbid any thing to be added. Such is the language held out to those who firmly believe all that is contained in Holy Scripture, or can be concluded and proved by the Scripture, and who have not forsaken, or denied, directly or by implication, an article of the faith which was taught by the Apostles of our Lord! I shall venture a few further general remarks on some part of the controversy, and so take leave of the subject.

1. I think we may observe, as an evil arising from forsaking the reasonable and godly ways of our Church, that converts to Rome commonly indulge in an amazing recklessness of statement. For example, in p. 61 of his first pamphlet, Mr. M. dilates on his favorite topic of the uncertainty in which Protestants must be left without an infallible guide, and permits himself to ask, "Why do Protestants reject the practice of *extreme unction*, as enjoined by St. James?" when it is notorious, that the unction to which St. James refers was connected with the miraculous healing of the sick, and that he does

not recommend it in the last hours of Christians. "The prayer of faith shall save the sick, and he shall recover." And again, "Why do Protestants reject the prohibition of the use of water by St. Paul?" A child could inform him that we do not require an infallible head to teach us that St. Paul did not forbid the general use of water. But where are his infallible directions on the same subject? The Church of Rome has not told him, whether he is to drink water only, or to "take a little wine," or to abstain from both. Such puerilities can serve no man's turn. But in his lecture on the origin of Christianity in England, his errors are of a graver kind. In perfect reliance on the ignorance of his readers, he quotes "the splendid testimony" of S. Irenæus to the Primacy of the See of Rome, in which he declares, "that with this Church, on account of her more powerful principality, it is necessary that every Church, that is the faithful on all sides, should agree, in which the Apostolical Tradition has been preserved by those who are on all sides." The translation is not very clear; but taking it as it stands, in order to establish Mr. Maturin's case, S. Irenæus should have said, that it was necessary to agree with the Roman Church on account of her *infallibility*, not on account of "*her more powerful principality*." But let us examine the original text, as far as we can, by quoting the ancient Latin translation of it, the Greek of S. Irenæus, in this place, having been lost: "Ad hanc enim ecclesiam, propter potentiorem principalitatem, necesse est omaem convenire Ecclesiam, hoc est, eos qui sunt undique fideles, in qua semper ab his qui sunt undique, conservata est ea quæ est ab Apostolis traditio." You will see at once, that Mr. Maturin has fallen into the grievous error of translating "convenire ad ecclesiam," as if it had been "consentire cum ecclesiâ," which is the more unpardonable, because it is simply transferring into the text of S. Irenæus the vain efforts of his commentator, Feuardentius, to make "*convenire*" signify the same with "*consentire*." It amounts, in fact, to an alteration of the text to prove his point. Again, the "undique fideles," is not the faithful on all sides, "ubi-que," but those who flock to Rome from every quarter, by whom even in Rome itself, S. Irenæus says, "the Apostolic tradition was preserved," which is a very different thing from representing Rome as mistress, and infallible teacher of all other Churches. But what is the substance of S. Irenæus' argument? He is shewing the extreme difficulty of dealing with the Valentinians, and other Gnostic heretics of his day. So slippery are they, says he, that if you appeal to Scripture, they meet you by exhibiting spurious Gospels, and quote them. If you appeal to tradition, they quote the genuine Scriptures, to prove that God has specially illuminated them, and that they are above tradition. Still we must use both methods, and after an abundant use of the Scriptural argument, which S. Irenæus is far from disclaiming, (as Mr. Maturin would have us believe,) S. Irenæus explains what he means by Tradition—not the oral testimony of individuals in opposition to their writings, "but a succession of Bishops from the times of the Apostles, who taught no such doctrine as the heretics pretend." Considering that S. Irenæus was the disciple of Polycarp, and Polycarp of St. John, and that he probably wrote this treatise about 60 or 70 years after St. John's death, his appeal to tradition is much as if we should appeal to what the Bishops of our Church generally said or taught in the middle, or towards the close of the reign of George the third, which would be no very difficult matter to ascertain. Now, says this holy father, " as it would be a tedious task to enumerate all the successive Bishops of every See in the world, we may apply ourselves to that famous Church founded by the blessed Apostles St. Peter and St. Paul, which holds the tradition from the Apostles, and the faith announced to mankind, by the succession of Bishops," in order to confound the Valentinian heresy. "For to this Church, by reason of its preeminence and power, the faithful must flock from every quarter," as the mother Church of all who reside in that part of the world, where the principal records are kept, by which the question may be decided. Here is indeed a "splendid" testimony to the primacy of the Church of Rome, such as we find it was! with which the argument of S. Irenæus had as much to do as Goodwin Sands with Tenterden steeple; for the sole question which S. Irenæus had in view was by what records the Valentinian heretics, who denied the true nature of Jesus Christ, might be shown to contradict the generally received doctrine of the Church. This has no reference to Roman supremacy, still less to the supremacy of the Roman Bishop, who is not even mentioned. On such mangled and supposititious evidence does our convert rest the strength of his cause. It should also be specially noticed that the Roman Bishop, when S. Irenæus wrote, could not possibly have had any " potentior principalitas," anything that could be called a dominion, under the reigns of the Emperors M. A. Antoninus, Commodus, and Severus. For the first three centuries, as is universally admitted, Christianity was scarcely tolerated in Rome.

2. I observe again, the extreme confusion that seems to pervade Mr. Maturin's mind on the subject of inspiration and infallibility. In his "Defence of the claims of the Catholic Church," (p. 68,) this strange note occurs, "Mr. Hunter asserts that St. Peter himself was not infallible. If so, it follows that his writings were not infallible; and if he was not infallible, it cannot surely be supposed that any other of the Apostles was infallible, and consequently their writings could not be infallible. Such a principle, then, tends directly to subvert the infallibility or inspiration of the Scriptures of the New Testament." Now, Mr. Hunter may very safely assert that St. Peter was not always infallible, when St. Paul himself says so, "When Peter was come to Antioch, I withstood him to the face, *because he was to be blamed.*" And when our Saviour says to him, after his famous confession of faith, "Get thee behind me Satan."* Mr. Maturin here confounds two very distinct things—the conduct of the Apostles considered as men and Christians, and their teaching considered as instruments of the Divine Spirit in making known a revelation. The Holy Ghost "spake in times past unto the prophets," who were all fallible men, but as teachers of revelation to mankind, infallibly inspired. Moses was fallible, for he once "spake unadvisedly with his lips;" David was fallible, for he fell into the sins of adultery and murder; Jonah was fallible, for he ran away from his duty; Balaam was not only fallible, but "perished in his iniquity;" and yet each and all of them spake, on certain occasions, by the unerring inspiration of the Holy Ghost. By admitting these undeniable facts, instead of undermining the authority of Scripture, we confirm the credit of the Book which records them. Inspiration does not confer infallibility except as regards the particular revelation which God saw fit to communicate by these several instruments to mankind. Apart from that inspiration, the human instrument becomes simply human, as liable to err, and as dependent on God's grace and help as any other human being. But is it not strange, that an infallible guide should not have been able to supply Mr. Maturin with less confused ideas than those on a subject so important as inspiration?

3. Mr. Maturin, following in the track of Bossuet, insists largely on the variations of Protestants, and on the impossibility of arriving at any certainty of faith, without the guidance of an infallible, living, earthly head of the Church. The first of these charges may be

* Galatians xx. 11. St. Matthew xvi. 23.

brought (as we all know) with equal force against Roman Catholics themselves. If these several infallible heads have notoriously differed from each other, in everything in which one man can differ from his fellow man—if they have denied each other's right to the Popedom—accused each other of the most frightful crimes—separated from each other at various times, carrying large portions of Christendom with them—if some of them have denounced as heresy what others of them have proclaimed as Christianity—if the whole his' ry of the Jesuits be a history of the opposition to the Popes, who alternately defended or accused, feared, or boasted of this powerful body, and one of whom, now denounced as a Simonist, suppressed it—with what confidence can we regard their decisions as infallible, or suppose that they can guarantee to us that certainty of faith, which, as a body, they evidently did not possess themselves? For had they possessed it they could not have differed so widely, and so implacably.

But we take wider ground than this. Is it part of the providential system of Divine Government, that a living, infallible, earthly head should preside over the destinies of the human race, and be the perpetual interpreter of his will to mankind? If the necessity for such an interpreter be supposed to arise from the weakness and ignorance of mankind, or from the obscurity of the Scriptures, is the Bible the only book open to this difficulty? All histories of past times, all accounts of foreign nations, oppose the same obstacles to human ignorance. Nay, our own mother tongue, as spoken or written several centuries ago, would be as unintelligible as a foreign language. But whither does this difficulty lead us? Do we suppose that a plain man cannot master the ordinary facts of English history, because every part of that history was originally written in Norman French, or Monkish Latin, or Anglo-Saxon? If this argument be used to imply the necessity of an infallible interpreter of Scripture, the same method of interpretation must be used for all history. For the Scripture presents no difficulties of interpretation, which do not apply (as far as the language is concerned) to every ancient document.

But perhaps it may be said, that the "oracles of God" require more than ordinary care, because our salvation is at stake, and a sound faith, as well as a holy practice, is required of us all. Here, then, we turn to the example of the Jewish Church. To it were "entrusted the oracles of God." But in what sense entrusted? Only as a keeper and a witness, not as an infallible interpreter. We

find from the book of Nehemiah; that when the Jews had in part
forgotten some of their ancient language, by reason of their long
captivity in Babylon, that Ezra explained and interpreted it to them.
"He read in the book, and gave them the sense, and caused them
to understand the reading."* But we fail in discovering any tokens
in the Hebrew records that the High Priests or Priests, as a successive body of men, were inspired by God, infallibly to interpret
his law. God indeed raised up a succession of prophets to interpret
his sacred oracles, and supply a new and enlarged revelation of his
will. But these appeared at vast intervals of time. After the days
of Joshua, we read of no such instances for nearly four centuries.
And after the days of Malachi, another pause occurs of four centuries. No trace appears of any one man or body of men being
commissioned by God perpetually and infallibly to interpret his
word, except the few persons who were inspired to write a revelation. And yet, if there were ever a time when we might have
expected to find a body of such interpreters, it would be before the
canon of Scripture was complete, in times of general ignorance
and corruption.

But, if such were the tenor of the New Testament covenant,
should we not expect to find it referred to in the epistles in plain
and unambiguous terms! The Apostles often refer to their own
inspiration. "Let him acknowledge," says St. Paul, "that the
things which I write unto you are the commandments of the Lord."†
"That ye may be mindful," says St. Peter, "of the words spoken
before by the Holy Prophets, and the commandments of us the
Apostles of the Lord and Saviour."‡ The only thing referred to is
"the teaching of the Prophets, and the commandments of the
Apostles." But although a whole chapter is devoted by St. Peter
to the denunciation of false teachers, not a hint is given of any infallible earthly guide to be continued after his decease, nor of any
one Church being the depository of this remarkable power. Is it
possible to believe, that if this power had been lodged with St.
Peter, as the head of the Roman Church, that he should have been
ignorant of it, and that neither himself nor any of his brother
Apostles should ever have alluded to it?

For, however, the charge given by our Saviour to St. Peter, may
be distorted into the claim of a prerogative, never claimed by the
Apostle, our opponent adds to this a claim which the text does not

---

* Nehemiah viii. 8.   † 1 Corinthians xiv. 37.   ‡ 2 Peter iii. 2.

give, the continuance of that power in the hands of the Bishops of Rome. Yet, against this we may fairly set the fact, that as far as we can see, St. Peter never advanced such a claim, never once exercised it, was never considered separately as an infallible head by the other Apostles, was publicly rebuked by one of them, was silent under the rebuke, and that in all the disputes which arose in the Apostolic age, no reference is made to the infallible authority of St. Peter *alone*, as sufficient to decide the question. But if St. Peter, and St. Peter only, above all the other Apostles, were not the depository of this infallible power of interpretation, with what face can the Bishop of Rome pretend to possess it? The whole supposition is grounded on two fallacies; first, the confounding inspiration (which is a special and particular grace vouchsafed not to Apostles alone, but to certain persons chosen by God to communicate his will to mankind) with a general infallibility given to a certain Church, and secondly, the confounding St. Peter's possession of this gift, *at certain periods of his life, when it pleased God to communicate to him a revelation of divine truth*, with the claim of the Bishops of Rome, to be the successive infallible interpreters of the original Revelation made known by all the Apostles, of which there is not the faintest trace in Scripture. But we may safely retort the argument of our opponent. You say that the Scriptures are obscure; that they are conveyed to mankind in languages of which the mass are ignorant; that the variations of interpretation are many; that the holy Word can only be guarded from corruption, and safely interpreted by the head of an infallible Church. How can you prove to us that we shall not misunderstand or misinterpret the decrees of the authority which you recommend? Where is it situated? In Italy. The power itself must speak to us through the medium of a foreign language. We must depend on translations. Even if the power be itself infallible, unless it can make us so too, it cannot guard us from errors incident to all mankind. And if mistakes can be still made, what advantage do we gain? The disadvantage is obvious, that we have two infallible authorities instead of one, both capable of being misunderstood: one in the written volume, the other in the living Pope; and they may not, and indeed do not always coincide.

St. Paul assures his son Timothy, that "all (or every) Scripture is divinely inspired, and profitable," not only profitable, but "able to make us wise unto salvation through faith which is in Christ

Jesus."* Admitting that St. Paul's primary reference may have been to the Old Testament Scriptures, yet both St. Matthew, St. Mark, and St. Luke, "whose praise is in the Gospel," had written their Gospels before St. Paul wrote to Timothy. But we learn from the second Epistle of St. Peter, that St. Paul's own Epistles (fourteen in number) were among those very Scriptures, which, "by the wisdom given unto him" by God, had been written for the common benefit of mankind. Consequently the expressions of St. Paul, by St. Peter's testimony, relate to his own Epistles as well as to the Old Testament, and if to St. Paul's Epistles, by parity of reasoning, to the other parts of the New Testament, which are therefore "able to make us wise unto salvation, through faith, as it is in Christ Jesus." So that, without asserting that every doctrine contained in Revelation is to be found in every book of Holy Scripture, it is evident, from the testimony of these two Apostles, that all that was known as Holy Scripture, contherm sufficiently all things necessary to salvation, and that we are referred to no other source. We admit that the teaching of St. Paul by word of mouth, was also able to make Timothy "wise unto salvation;" but such oral instructions no longer exist; the record of them in the Scriptures is all that are now remaining, and as that record contains no reference to the preservation of his oral teaching by any other method, we are not justified in expecting it to come from any other person.

We fully admit that our faith is built on the sense, not on the syllables of Scripture. But God's Revelation is committed to the keeping of fallible beings, and is communicated (even by the admission of our adversaries) through a fallible medium, that of language; and unless both the teacher and the disciple be rendered infallible, it would be as easy to mistake or pervert the sense of an infallible living guide, as to pervert the sense of an infallible written volume. Thus, even if we had what it is pretended we must have, in order to a certain faith and an assured hope of salvation, we should be no better with it than without it, for we should have no more than we have at present—*infallible directions capable of misconstruction and perversion.*

But what if the possessors of this supposed infallibility of interpretation do not themselves agree? What if Popes contradict and even excommunicate each other? What if three persons at once

---

* 2 Timothy iii. 16.

lay claim to this power, each contending that the others are not entitled to it ! What if that which one Pope solemnly and repeat-
edly declares to be a mark of Antichrist, another as unhesitatingly
declares to be " necessary to everlasting salvation ?" We may meet
with difficulties in Scripture ; we meet with variations amongst ourselves ; but not with such discrepancies as these : because we admit
our infallibility, which the Popes do not. To say nothing of the
fact, that the precise seat of the infallible power is not agreed upon
by Romanists themselves.

We do not (in the Church of England at least) admit that each
individual is left to discover his faith for himself. Whilst we refer
for the great foundation and proof of all we believe to the Word of
God alone, we thankfully embrace that which has large, credible,
and convincing guarantees of its being agreeable to the Word of
God, from the general belief and consent of the Christian world ;
and we point with satisfaction to the fact, that all that we believe
is to be found in the writings of the primitive Church, and was de-
duced by them from the Scripture, and that even by the confession
of our adversaries, several articles of their faith were not defined as
articles of faith, till a very late period, one, indeed, not six years
ago. Let them name one ancient creed of the three first centuries,
which contains the doctrines now set forth by them as necessary to
salvation, and they will have made a stronger point than any which
they have yet established in this controversy.

4. On one point, Mr. Maturin prudently says but little : the ex-
cessive and unscriptural expressions of trust, confidence, and adora-
ration applied to the Virgin Mary. Numerous testimonies to this
effect are cited in Dr. Gray's pamphlet ; but as Roman Catholics
continually deny that such expressions are commonly used, I can
myself bear testimony to having examined one of their ordinary
books of devotion, for the Holy Communion, circulated in this Province, professedly taken from the writings of Liguori. In that work,
all the expressions which a pious Christian usually applies to our Saviour, such as " our trust, our hope, our salvation," and many others,
were applied without scruple to the blessed Virgin ; nor was it easy
to discover in what respect but that of sex, the mother of our Saviour
differed from the Supreme God. Not an intimation was given of the
feeling of the writer, that the mother of our Lord owed her salvation
to the merits of her Divine Son ; but the attention of the communicant was directed, for whole pages, to the merit, greatness, majesty,
and influence of the Virgin herself, sometimes without one qualifying

expression, at most, with the qualification of benefits being gained by her intercession, even this but seldom. And as Liguori is a canonized Saint, this work is, of course, a work of authority.

This one feature of modern Romanism is sufficient, with me, to regard it as thoroughly uncatholic and unscriptural. For it is perfectly incredible, that if such a system had been agreeable to the mind and will of God, no reference should have been made to it in one of the Epistles of St. Paul, St. Peter, St. James, or St. John, nor one single hope expressed by them for the intercession of the Virgin Mary. How could they have wholly passed by so essential and fundamental a doctrine, if true, whilst not a document is ever put forth by the modern Pope without some reference to it? But I must not detain you longer on this subject, on which I should not have said so much, but for the confident tone and daring assertions of the clergyman who is unhappily involved in all these gross and frightful errors, and has bound himself to believe them all. May God bring him, as he has brought many others, to see his mistake, and to acknowledge publicly that he did not find the unity and truth which he expected. As regards these secessions, I am assured that there is scarce one among the clergy, which has not arisen from a morbid and exclusive dwelling on the faults of members of our own Church, without considering what is to be said on the other side, and from reading Roman Catholic works of devotion. And if they can count their converts by hundreds, we can claim our's by thousands. But this kind of boasting is not very creditable to either party. Let Church of England parents see to it, that they carefully train their children in strict Church of England principles, and set them a sound and wholesome example of conformity to the rules of our Church, and of steadfast support of her clergy and institutions, and I have no fear that they will be seduced into Romanism. The best safeguard against all these errors, is not ill-grounded and frantic abuse of Roman Catholics as a body, but the possession of distinct and clear notions on the fulness of truth, which it has pleased God to vouchsafe to ourselves. Continued and measured abuse of any party will be apt to incline ingenuous minds to look on it with favour; whereas the calm consciousness of possessing true Church privileges, of enjoying rational freedom, with a wholesome restraint of individual license, and every guarantee for the fixedness and stability of our faith, will help us to continue steadfast, and will attract those to us who are capable of being won by such persuasions.

I gladly turn, in conclusion, to a more congenial subject, and would offer some advice on the best method of increasing and extending the missionary spirit of our Church among ourselves.

First—It is absolutely indispensable that we should all accustom ourselves to look on all Church members in every part of the Province as one body. One mode of action will be preferred to another by various minds, labouring for the same end; but we should at least give each other credit for the same intention, whatever be the mode of action. No real Church unity can be understood, unless we so far abandon party names and distinctions, as not to speak unkindly of our brethren, lay or clerical, and not to hold them up to public odium, because they differ from us. There has been an evil habit of stigmatizing good men in our Church, by assigning to them names which they disavow. It is an evil habit, and it is a cowardly habit; for it is generally done by persons to whom it is impossible to reply. If we really mean to do any thing good for the Church of England, it is high time that this custom should cease.

Secondly—It is very desirable that a general registry should be established of all our Church members, that we may know more accurately both our strength and our weakness. In every Parish a book should be kept of persons in general attendance, and in full communion with the Church, which should be the property of the Parish, and be left by each clergyman to the care of his successor. Each parishioner should be invited to register his name, and that of his family, when they are Church people, in this book.

Thirdly—Every member of the Church should be now convinced, that on him lies the duty of maintaining and extending it to the utmost of his means, by his prayers, his influence, and his contributions, and that he should lay aside a stated part of his income for religious and charitable purposes, amongst which must be named, the support of the parochial clergy. This duty ought not henceforth to be devolved on charitable societies in England, nor on the rich in New Brunswick, but on *the members of the Church*, considered as a whole. It must be recollected, that the relation of the labourer to his employer, is very different here from that which subsists in the mother-country, and that those who obtain four times as much wages for their work as in England, can no longer claim to be exempt from the duty of contributing to the clergy, because in fact they are richer than the clergy. They have, in many instances, larger incomes, with far fewer claims. And, again, in these instances in which capital, skill, and industry have accumulated large properties, it must be borne in mind that these properties cannot (according to the express word of God) be lawfully or safely used and enjoyed, unless a liberal share be given to the Church of God. And a liberal share is not a few superfluous pounds flung under the table, like the crumbs that were given at the feast of Dives, but a really large pecuniary offering, made in the fear of God, and in the solemn remembrance of that dreadful account which those "who trust in riches" will soon have to give before Almighty God. The offering must be large, liberal, and annual, if the means of giving be continued, and the proportion is sufficiently indicated in Scripture, which strongly recommends that a tenth of our income should be devoted to religious and charitable uses. And the exemption from the temporal law of tithes is no reason why we should not comply with a Scriptural injunction, with the law of God, which would stand, and be in force, if there were no State-laws in existence in any part of the world.

Fourthly—We require not only larger contributions, but a larger Missionary spirit. To this end, the Church in New Brunswick should consider itself as part of a great Missionary Association, divinely organized and set in motion by the Church at home. To assist in promoting this good spirit, which lies at the very root of all Christianity, (for what is "thy kingdom come," but a prayer for Missions and Missionaries,) I propose :*

1. That every father of a family, and every individual not placed in that relation, should add to his own daily private prayers, some one special prayer in behalf of Missions, including those in other countries, and those in this Diocese. This may be either the Collect for Good Friday, which is one of the best we can use, or any other suitable prayer, but the simpler the better.

2. That the Clergy should agree once a year, either on or near to the Festival of the Epiphany, the conversion of St. Paul, or Whitsunday, or one of the Advent Sundays, or any more suitable time hereafter to be agreed upon, (but it would be desirable to agree on some one time,) to urge on their parishioners the duty of Missionary efforts, and should bring the subject strongly before them, holding a Missionary meeting in the week following, if convenient. The attention of the whole Church would then be drawn

---

* I gladly adopt the substance of these propositions, first made in a contemporary Review.

to the same important subject. Cheap and useful publications, such as the "Gospel Messenger," the "Mission Field," and others, might easily be obtained.

3. About the same time, the Lord's Supper might be celebrated in every principal Church, and it might be enjoined on every communicant to make the work of Missions the subject of thankful prayer, in connexion with the memorial of the death of our Lord, and of the benefits we receive by the Lord's Supper, with a special petition for the enlargement of the Redeemer's kingdom in this Province.

4. Collections might also be made to promote Missionary work. Thus, listlessness, apathy and inactivity would be dispelled; charity and good feeling would be every where promoted. Intercessory prayer for the conversion of the heathen, for our own special Church, for more unity on Scriptural principles, and for all needful blessings, would be increased. And we should, "with one mind and one mouth, glorify God, even the Father of our Lord Jesus Christ." By this godly method, no interference is intended with any shades of opinion, or difference of practice, but we are invited to join in general Christian duties, in which we must all agree, if we take the Word of God for our guide, whatever be our differences on particular questions. And till we learn to dwell more on the points of agreement than on points of difference, we shall know little of the true purity, truth and love of the Gospel of Christ.

And let me urge upon you once more, reverend and dear brethren, the duty of combining in humble and hearty prayer to the Father of our Lord Jesus Christ, that He would be pleased to grant a larger measure of His Holy Spirit, to guide us in these and in all our undertakings. We read much every where of the outpouring of the Holy Spirit in answer to prayer. But for us, who enjoy the benefit of continual supplications, in the Liturgy, it is not necessary to resort to any extraordinary measures and violent excitements for this end. Guiding ourselves by the standard of the New Testament, we read there, that the measures of the primitive Church were as calm and collected as they were energetic, and that wisdom and prudence are as much the gifts of the Spirit of God, as repentance and faith. We have in our own Church all the gifts and appliances that are needed, or can be devised. We have an ancient and primitive faith, a common, godly, Scriptural, elevated form of worship, a translation of the Scriptures, distinguished for its general fidelity and purity, and unrivalled for its melody and sweetness. We

F

have an Apostolic form of government, and a sacred literature, unsurpassed in masculine strength, and variety of information, by that of any nation on earth. We have examples in abundance, of men most learned, most godly, most charitable and devout, gifted with rare genius and admirable eloquence, rejoicing in our Communion, and spending their lives in its defence. We have poetry, architecture, music, largely enrolled on our side. Our only implacable foe is IGNORANCE. The more widely sound knowledge of all kinds is extended, the more deeply and learnedly the Scriptures and Church history are examined, the more thorough and entire is the education of the people at large, the more numerous will be (I believe) the converts to the Church of England. And the more the great question between us and Rome is sifted, the wider will spread the conviction among educated men, that the Church of England, or some body of like principles and aims, can alone be their defender from the depths of prevailing unbelief—unbelief which is no where more prevalent than in the chief seats of the Roman dominion.

All that we require, is to use such high gifts aright; humbly, faithfully, unitedly, continually. Let us all make this use of them at the several services of this Visitation. Let us endeavour to carry home with us the savour of them into our parochial cures. Let it be our chief desire, by the wisdom, humility, steadfastness and simplicity of our own course, to win others to the truth, and to make those who nominally belong to us, more firm, stable, and consistent members of the Church of England, resting their adherence to it, their support of it, their belief in its doctrines and discipline, on its being agreeable to the word of God, and to Catholic truth, as taught by the primitive Church, and freed from the extremes of irreverence and superstition. Let us not aim at making men admirers of ourselves, but servants and worshippers of the Lord; that we may grow in holiness, live in unity, meet in peace, differ (if need be) in charity, suffer in patience, labour in constancy, die in hope of rising in glory. And when all our work is ended, may we all be "for ever with the Lord." Let us "comfort one another" with such words.

Note.—Having been accused of libelling the Rev. J. Wesley, for quoting as his words, "I fear when the Methodists leave the Church, God will leave them," I now mention, that this quotation is found in a tract published at Leeds, and by Rivingtons, London, and the words alluded to, have appended to them, "*Minutes of Conference*, 1770." Whether Mr. Wesley was the first who used these expressions, I am not at present able to say. There is, however, no reason to doubt that they were used by a clergyman who was a member of his Society; that they were mentioned by Mr. Wesley without disapproval, and that he added to them "other like words."

The following extracts from Mr. Wesley's works have been verified by a friend in England :—

"Are we not, unawares, by little and little, sliding into a separation from the Church? O, remove every tendency thereto with all diligence. Let all our preachers go to Church. Let all the people go constantly. Warn them against despising the prayers of the Church. *Against calling our Society a Church, the Church*. Against calling our Preachers Ministers, our houses meeting houses; call them simply preaching houses. They that leave the Church, leave the Methodists." Works, vol. 6. It is almost needless to add, that Mr. Wesley meant by "the Church," the Church of England, as this was the usual way of speaking in his time.

Again, "I never had any design of separating from the Church. I have no such design now. I do, and will do, all in my power to prevent such an event. Nevertheless, in spite of all I can do, many of them will separate from it. *In flat opposition to these, I declare once more, that I live and die a member of the Church of England; and that none who regard my judgment or advice, will ever separate from it.*" Dec. 1789. This shows in what sense he used the words "the Church," cited before.

Again, 1787. Extract from his last journal. "I went over to Deptford, but it seemed I had got into a den of lions. Most of the leading men of the Society were mad for separating from the Church. I endeavoured to reason with them, but they had neither sense nor good manners left. At length, after meeting the whole Society, I told them, if you are resolved, you may have your service in Church hours; but remember, from that time you will see my face no more. This struck deep, and from that time I have heard no more of separating from the Church."

The above extracts are sufficient for my purpose, which is not to attack any party not in communion with the Church of England, but to defend myself against the charge of misrepresenting Mr. Wesley's real sentiments.